달밤

아시아에서는 《바이링궐 에디션 한국 대표 소설》을 기획하여 한국의 우수한 문학을 주제별로 엄선해 국내외 독자들에게 소개합니다. 이 기획은 국내외 우수한 번역가들이 참여하여 원작의 품격을 최대한 살렸습니다. 문학을 통해 아시아의 정체성과 가치를 살피는 데 주력해 온 아시아는 한국인의 삶을 넓고 깊게 이해하는 데 이 기획이 기여하기를 기대합니다.

Asia Publishers presents some of the very best modern Korean literature to readers worldwide through its new Korean literature series 〈Bilingual Edition Modern Korean Literature〉. We are proud and happy to offer it in the most authoritative translation by renowned translators of Korean literature. We hope that this series helps to build solid bridges between citizens of the world and Koreans through a rich in-depth understanding of Korea.

바이링궐 에디션 한국 대표 소설 098

Bi-lingual Edition Modern Korean Literature 098

An Idiot's Delight

이태준
달밤

Yi T'ae-jun

ASIA
PUBLISHERS

Contents

달밤

An Idiot's Delight

성북동(城北洞)으로 이사 나와서 한 대엿새 되었을까, 그날 밤 나는 보던 신문을 머리맡에 밀어 던지고 누워 새삼스럽게,

　"여기도 정말 시골이로군!"

하였다.

　무어 바깥이 컴컴한 걸 처음 보고 시냇물 소리와 쏴
― 하는 솔바람 소리를 처음 들어서가 아니라 황수건이라는 사람을 이날 저녁에 처음 보았기 때문이다.

　그는 말 몇 마디 사귀지 않아서 곧 못난이란 것이 드러났다. 이 못난이는 성북동의 산들보다 물들보다 조그만 지름길들보다 더 나에게 성북동이 시골이란 느낌을

"Just like the countryside," I said to myself as I pushed aside my newspaper and lay down in bed. It was several days after we'd arrived in Seongbuk-dong, on the outskirts of Seoul.

It wasn't my initial sight of the dark shapes outside our door, nor was it the chittering of the stream or the sighing of the wind in the pine trees that gave me this feeling, but rather the sight of that man Hwang Su-gŏn.

With only a few words he had given himself away as a simpleton. More than the hills near our new home in Seongbuk-dong, more than the brooks and the shortcuts, it was this simpleton who filled

풍겨주었다.

서울이라고 못난이가 없을 리야 없겠지만 대처에서는 못난이들이 거리에 나와 행세를 하지 못하고, 시골에선 아무리 못난이라도 마음 놓고 나와 다니는 때문인지, 못난이는 시골에만 있는 것처럼 흔히 시골에서 잘 눈에 뜨인다. 그리고 또 흔히 그는 태고 때 사람처럼 그 우둔하면서도 천진스런 눈을 가지고, 자기 동리에 처음 들어서는 손에게 가장 순박한 시골의 정취를 돋워 주는 것이다.

그런데 그날 밤 황수건이는 열 시나 되어서 우리 집을 찾아왔다.

그는 어두운 마당에서 꽥 지르는 소리로,

"아, 이 댁이 문안서……."

하면서 들어섰다. 잡담 제하고 큰일이나 난 사람처럼 건넌방 문 앞으로 달려들더니,

"저, 저 문안 서대문 거리라나요, 어디선가 나오신 댁입쇼?"

한다.

보니 핫삐[1]는 안 입었으되 신문을 들고 온 것이 신문 배달부다.

me with the feeling that I was in rustic surroundings.

Of course there's no reason to presume that big
cities lack simpletons. It's just that in an urban cen-
ter you don't see them on the street. In the countryside, though, any sort of fool can go about free
as the wind. And this is probably the reason simpletons are often in view there, giving one the im-
pression that rural areas are the only places they're
found. They often have the obtuse, artless look of
people from bygone eras, and to someone who
enters a village for the first time, this look gives rise
to a mood of unspoiled rusticity.

Anyway, it wasn't a week since we had moved to
Seongbuk-dong that Hwang paid us a visit. It was
about ten in the evening when I heard a shout from
the gloom of our courtyard:

"Are you the folks who moved out here from the
city?"

Dispensing with preliminaries, he jumped up onto
the veranda and rushed over to the lattice door of
my study like someone in a heap of trouble.

"I heard you folks are from the West Gate area."

The newspapers he was toting suggested he was
a paperboy, though he wasn't wearing the uniform.

"그렇소, 신문이오?"

"아, 그런 걸 사흘이나 저, 저 건너 쪽에만 가 찾었습죠. 제기……."

하더니 신문을 방에 들이뜨리며,

"그런뎁쇼, 왜 이렇게 죄꼬만 집을 사구 와곕쇼. 아, 내가 알었더면 이 아래 큰 개와집도 많은걸입쇼……."

한다. 하 말이 황당스러워 유심히 그의 생김을 내다보니 눈에 얼른 두드러지는 것이 빡빡 깎은 머리로되 보통 크다는 정도 이상으로 골이 크다. 그런데다 옆으로 보니 장구 대가리다.

"그렇소? 아무튼 집 찾느라고 수고했소."

하니 그는 큰 눈과 큰 입이 일시에 히죽거리며,

"뭘입쇼, 이게 제 업인뎁쇼."

하고 날래 물러서지 않고 목을 길게 빼어 방 안을 살핀다. 그러더니 묻지도 않는데,

"저는입쇼, 이 동네 사는 황수건이라 합니다……."

하고 인사를 붙인다. 나도 깍듯이 내 성명을 대었다. 그는 또 싱글벙글하면서,

"댁엔 개가 없구먼입쇼."

한다.

"Well, so you deliver the paper?"

"Oh, this—three days now I been searching for you folks across the way there. Darn!" He threw a paper into my study. "How come you folks bought such a tiny house, anyhow? I could of told you there's a lot of big houses with tile roofs down thataway..."

Somewhat taken aback by his audacity, I examined his features. What struck me about him was his cropped hair and his bulging, oversize head.

"Is that so? Well, anyway, thanks for taking the trouble to find us."

This brought a contented smile to his face. "Thanks for what? It's my job."

But instead of leaving, he craned his neck and inspected the study. Then, without any prompting, he introduced himself.

"Hwang Su-gŏn—that's me. I'm one of your neighbors."

I politely told him my name, and he produced another grin.

"You folks own a dog?"

"No. Not yet, anyway."

"Please don't."

"Why not?"

"아직 없소."

하니,

"개 그까짓 거 두지 마십쇼."

한다.

"왜 그렇소?"

물으니, 그는 얼른 대답하는 말이,

"신문 보는 집엔입쇼, 개를 두지 말아야 합니다."

한다. 이것 재미있는 말이다 하고 나는,

"왜 그렇소?"

하고 또 물었다.

"아, 이 뒷동네 은행소에 댕기는 집엔입쇼, 망아지만
한 개가 있는뎁쇼, 아, 신문을 배달할 수가 있어얍죠."

"왜?"

"막 깨물랴고 덤비는걸입쇼."

한다. 말 같지 않아서 나는 웃기만 하니 그는 더욱 신을
낸다.

"그눔의 개 그저, 한번, 양떡을 멕여 대야 할 텐
데……."

하면서 주먹을 부르대는데 보니, 손과 팔목은 머리에
비기어 반비례로 작고 가느다랗다.

14

"I have to ask all the folks on my route not to," he quickly replied.

I found this rather intriguing, so I asked him again to explain.

"Well, there's a bank clerk in the next neighborhood back that has a dog the size of a pony. How's a fellow supposed to deliver a paper to a place like that?"

"What's the problem?"

"The thing'll sink its teeth into me."

I couldn't quite see that as a necessary consequence, and I smiled. This made Hwang even more animated.

"Damn dog. I'll learn him a lesson one of these days."

He brandished a fist, and I noticed that his hands and wrists were as small and slender as his head was large and bulging.

"You must have had a long day. Isn't it time you went home and got some rest?"

Hwang reluctantly got up and took his leave.

"Good night, Mr. Yi, sir. We don't live too far from you."

Although he now knew where we lived, it was after nine when he appeared the following evening.

15

"어서 곤할 텐데 가 자시오."

하니 그는 마지못해 물러서며,

"선생님, 참 이 선생님 편안히 주무쇼. 저이 집은 여기서 얼마 안 되는 걸입쇼."

하더니 돌아갔다.

그는 이튿날 저녁, 집을 알고 오는데도 아홉 시가 지나서야,

"신문 배달해 왔습니다."

하고 소리를 치며 들어섰다.

"오늘은 왜 늦었소?"

물으니,

"자연 그럽죠."

하고 다른 이야기를 꺼냈다.

자기는 워낙 이 아래 있는 삼산학교에서 일을 보다 어떤 선생하고 뜻이 덜 맞아 나왔다는 것, 지금은 신문 배달을 하나 원배달이 아니라 보조 배달이라는 것, 저희 집엔 양친과 형님 내외와 조카 하나와 저의 내외까지 식구가 일곱이라는 것, 저의 아버지와 저의 형님의 이름은 무엇무엇이며, 자기 이름은 황가인 데다가 목숨 수(壽) 자하고 세울 건(建) 자로 황수건이기 때문에, 아

"Here's your paper!" he shouted as he entered the front gate.

"Why so late?" I asked.

"Because." And then he changed the subject.

Originally he had worked at Samsan Primary School, some distance down the hill, he proceeded to inform me. But then he had some trouble with a teacher there. And now he was delivering newspapers, but he wasn't a regular carrier, only a helper. His family consisted of his parents, his older brother and his wife, a niece, and him and his wife—a grand total of seven. And his father's name was such-and-such, his brother's name so-and-so. His family name was Hwang; his given name was Sugǒn, whose two elements meant "life" and "construct." But because *Hwang* means "yellow" and the word *sugǒn* means "towel," the children teased him by calling him Yellow Towel, and this was how he was known by all the families in Seongbuk-dong. All of this he related proudly.

Again it became necessary for me to break in: "I think the neighbors are waiting for their papers."

He left reluctantly.

My wife would ask me what I was talking about with "that halfwit," but I must admit I enjoyed gab-

이들이 노랑 수건이라고 놀리어서 성북동에서는 가가
호호에서 노랑 수건 하면, 다 자긴 줄 알리라고 자랑스
럽게 이야기하다가 이날도,

"어서 그만 다른 집에도 신문을 갖다 줘야 하지 않
소?"

하니까 그때서야 마지못해 나갔다.

우리 집에서는 그까짓 반편[2]과 무얼 대구를 해 가지
고 그러느냐 하되, 나는 그와 지껄이기가 좋았다.

그는 아무것도 아닌 것을 가지고 열심스럽게 이야기
하는 것이 좋았고, 그와는 아무리 오래 지껄이어도 힘
이 들지 않고, 또 아무리 오래 지껄이고 나도 웃음밖에
는 남는 것이 없어 기분이 거든해지는 것도 좋았다. 그
래서 나는 무슨 일을 하는 중만 아니면 한참씩 그의 말
을 받아주었다.

어떤 날은 서로 말이 막히기도 했다. 대답이 막히는
것이 아니라 무슨 말을 해야 할까 하고 막히었다. 그러
나 그는 늘 나보다 빠르게 이야깃거리를 잘 찾아냈다.
오뉴월인데도 "꿩고기를 잘 먹느냐?"고도 묻고, "양복은
저고리를 먼저 입느냐, 바지를 먼저 입느냐?"고도 묻고
"소와 말과 싸움을 붙이면 어느 것이 이기겠느냐?"는

bing with him. I liked the enthusiastic way he talked about the most trivial things, and we could chatter on for the longest time without any effort on my part. And no matter how long he carried on, I was always left with a good laugh, which lightened my heart. So I always took the time to chat with him if I wasn't in the middle of something important.

Sometimes our exchanges proceeded in fits and starts—not because we couldn't answer each other's questions, but because we couldn't always find something suitable to talk about. But when it came to launching in on a new topic, he did a better job than I. It might be May or June, but he'd ask me if I liked pheasant—something people ate only in winter. A couple of my other favorites were, "When you're wearing a Western suit, what do you put on first, the jacket or the pants?" and "If a cow and a horse got into a fight, who do you think would win?" No matter what we talked about, he would come up with something quite original. I couldn't help but be impressed by the range of his remarks.

One day I asked him what he wanted to do in life.

"Piece of cake—I want to be a regular paperboy."

He was now making three *wŏn* or so a month for delivering twenty or so copies for the regular carri-

둥, 아무튼 그가 얘깃거리를 취재하는 방면은 기상천외로 여간 범위가 넓지 않은 데는 도저히 당할 수가 없었다. 하루는 나는 "평생소원이 무엇이냐?"고 그에게 물어보았다. 그는 "그까짓 것쯤 얼른 대답하기는 누워서 떡 먹기"라고 하면서 평생소원은 자기도 원배달이 한번 되었으면 좋겠다는 것이었다.

남이 혼자 배달하기 힘들어서 한 이십 부 떼어주는 것을 배달하고 월급이라고 원배달에게서 한 삼 원 받는 터이라, 월급을 이십여 원을 받고 신문사 옷을 입고 방울을 차고 다니는 원배달이 제일 부럽노라 하였다. 그리고 방울만 차면 자기도 뛰어다니며 빨리 돌릴 뿐 아니라 그 은행소에 다니는 집 개도 조금도 무서울 것이 없겠노라 하였다.

그래서 나는 "그럴 것 없이 아주 신문사 사장쯤 되었으면 원배달도 바랄 것 없고 그 은행소에 다니는 집 개도 상관할 바 없지 않겠느냐?" 한즉 그는 뚱그래지는 눈알을 한참 굴리며 생각하더니 "딴은 그렇겠다"고 하면서, 자기는 경난이 없어 거기까지는 바랄 생각도 못 하였다고 무릎을 치듯 가슴을 쳤다.

그러나 신문 사장은 이내 잊어버리고 원배달만 마음

er. Naturally, the position of a regular, which paid upwards of twenty *wŏn* in addition to the uniform and bell the company issued you, was the most enviable thing in the world. All he'd have to do was ring that bell, he said, and he'd make his rounds in a jiffy, plus that dog at the bank clerk's house wouldn't faze him a bit.

"Why not shoot for president of the whole newspaper, or something like that? Then you could forget about being a regular paperboy, and you wouldn't have to worry about that dog, would you?"

Su-gŏn rolled those round eyes of his, thought for a minute, and said, "Indeed." For lack of worldly experience that thought had never entered his mind, he said, pounding on his chest the way other people might slap their knee.

But he soon forgot about the idea of president and fixed his sights on becoming a regular carrier. And then one day we heard him shout from the courtyard:

"Mr. Yi! Oh, Mr. Yi! I'll be a regular starting tomorrow. Just think, I'll wake up tomorrow morning and..."

I asked for particulars.

Seongbuk-dong had been made a separate route,

에 박혔던 듯, 하루는 바깥마당에서부터 무어라고 떠들어 대며 들어왔다.

"이 선생님? 이 선생님 곕쇼? 아, 저도 내일부턴 원배달이올시다. 오늘 밤만 자면입쇼……."

한다. 자세히 물어보니 성북동이 따로 한 구역이 되었는데, 자기가 맡게 되었으니까 내일은 배달복을 입고 방울을 막 떨렁거리면서 올 테니 보라고 한다. 그리고 "사람이란 게 그러게 무어든지 끝을 바라고 붙들어야 한다"고 나에게 일러주면서 신이 나서 돌아갔다.

우리도 그가 원배달이 된 것이 좋은 친구가 큰 출세나 하는 것처럼 마음속으로 진실로 즐거웠다. 어서 내일 저녁에 그가 배달복을 입고 방울을 차고 와서 쩔렁거리는 것을 보리라 하였다.

그러나 이튿날 그는 오지 않았다. 밤이 늦도록 신문도 그도 오지 않았다. 그다음 날도 신문도 그도 오지 않다가 사흘째 되는 날에야, 이날은 해도 지기 전인데 방울소리가 요란스럽게 우리 집으로 뛰어들었다.

"어디 보자!"

he told me, and the next day he'd drop by so we could see him in uniform ringing his bell. "Keep your nose to the grindstone—it always pays off," he philosophized. Then he left in high spirits.

We were as delighted as if a good friend had achieved a great success. We looked forward to seeing him swagger in the next evening wearing his uniform and ringing his bell.

But he didn't return the next day. We waited until late in the evening, but neither he nor the paper arrived. The following day was the same. Finally, on the third day, long before sunset, the clamor of the bell raced into our house.

"Let's have a look at this!" I said as I rushed outside.

But the figure in the uniform with the bell and the newspapers was not Hwang Su-gŏn but rather someone I had never seen before.

"Did you take over for the other fellow?" I asked.

"Yes, I'm in charge of Seongbuk-dong now."

"Was the other fellow assigned somewhere else?"

"I'm not sure where they'd want a nincompoop like that," the man said with a smile. "They were going to use him as a paperboy, but it seems they changed their minds when they found out how

하고 나는 방에서 뛰어나갔다.

　그러나 웬일일까, 정말 배달복에 방울을 차고 신문을 들고 들어서는 사람은 황수건이가 아니라 처음 보는 사람이다.

　"왜 전엣사람은 어디 가고 당신이오?"

물으니 그는,

　"제가 성북동을 맡았습니다."

한다.

　"그럼, 전엣사람은 어디를 맡았소?"

하니 그는 픽 웃으며,

　"그까짓 반편을 어딜 맡깁니까? 배달부로 쓸랴다가 똑똑지가 못하니까 안 쓰고 말었나 봅니다."

한다.

　"그럼 보조 배달도 떨어졌소?"

하니,

　"그럼요, 여기가 따루 한 구역이 된걸이오."

하면서 방울을 울리며 나갔다.

　이렇게 되었으니 황수건이가 우리 집에 올 길은 없어지고 말았다. 나도 가끔 문안엔 다니지만 그의 집은 내가 다니는 길옆은 아닌 듯 길가에서도 잘 보이지 않았다.

dumb he is."

"So he's not even a helper?"

"That's right. Seongbuk-dong is a route by itself now, and I don't need help."

With a ring of his bell the man was off.

And so Hwang Su-gŏn no longer had occasion to visit us. I occasionally went into town, but his house didn't seem to be on my way, because I never ran into him.

It was as if a close friend had been sent far away, or had failed in a large-scale business venture, and I wouldn't be seeing him again. Indeed, my heart ached. The world had treated Su-gŏn heartlessly, and I resented that.

As Su-gŏn had said, he was well known throughout the neighborhood as Yellow Towel. I gradually realized that anyone who had lived in Seongbuk-dong for any length of time would smile at the mention of his name.

From my short association with him I had gathered he would be full of humorous anecdotes about himself. There were numerous stories from his days as an errand boy at Samsan School. Let me pass along a couple that circulated among the neighbors. The one I found most delightful was

나는 가까운 친구를 먼 곳에 보낸 것처럼, 아니 친구가 큰 사업에나 실패하는 것을 보는 것처럼, 못 만나는 섭섭뿐이 아니라 마음이 아프기도 하였다. 그 당자와 함께 세상의 야박함이 원망스럽기도 하였다.

한데 황수건은 그의 말대로 노랑 수건이라면 온 동네에서 유명은 하였다. 노랑 수건 하면 누구나 성북동에서 오래 산 사람이면 먼저 웃고 대답하는 것을 나는 차츰 알았다.

내가 잠깐씩 며칠 보기에도 그랬거니와 그에겐 우스운 일화도 한두 가지가 아니었다.

삼산학교에 급사로 있을 시대에 삼산학교에다 남겨 놓고 나온 일화도 여러 가지라는데, 그중에 두어 가지를 동네 사람들의 말대로 옮겨보면, 역시 그때부터도 이야기하기를 대단 즐기어 선생들이 교실에 들어간 새 손님이 오면 으레 손님을 앉히고는 자기도 걸상을 갖다 떡 마주 놓고 앉는 것은 물론, 마주 앉아서는 곧 자기류의 만담 삼매로 빠지는 것인데, 한번은 도 학무국에서 시학관이 나온 것을 이 따위로 대접하였다. 일본 말을 못 하니까 만담은 할 수 없고 마주 앉아서 자꾸 일본 말을 연습하였다.

this:

If a visitor arrived when the teachers were in class, Su-gŏn would offer him a seat, sit down across from him, and devote himself to entertaining the guest in his own comic way. Once he had received an inspector from the provincial bureau of education and management in this fashion. The man was a Japanese, but Su-gŏn didn't know enough of the language to perform his usual antic routine, and so he proceeded to practice what little Japanese he knew.

"*Sensei,* heh-heh, *ohayo gozaimasu ka,* heh-heh, *ame ga hurimasu. Yuki ga hurimasu ka,* heh-heh..."

The official smiled the first time he heard this, but by the tenth or twentieth time he wasn't so pleased. The teachers kept waiting for the bell to end class, and finally one of them emerged from his classroom to find that Su-gŏn had forgotten this duty of his and was sitting directly across from his guest reciting, "*Ohayo. Yuki ga hurimasu ka...*"

That day, Su-gŏn was soundly reprimanded by the teachers, and he promised not to repeat this behavior. But he wasn't able to break himself of his habit, and in the end he was discharged by the school.

"센세이 히, 오하요 고자이마쓰까(선생님, 안녕하십니까)?…… 히히 아메가 후리마쓰(비가 옵니다). 유끼가 후리마쓰까(눈이 옵니까)? 히히……."

시학관도 인정이라 처음엔 웃었다. 그러나 열 번 스무번을 되풀이하는 데는 성이 나고 말았다. 선생들은 아무리 기다려도 종소리가 나지 않으니까, 한 선생이 나와 보니 종 칠 것도 잊어버리고 손님과 마주 앉아서 "오하요 유끼가 후리마쓰까……" 하는 판이다.

그날 수건이는 선생들에게 단단히 몰리고 다시는 안 그러겠노라고 했으나, 그 버릇을 고치지 못해서 그예 쫓겨 나오고 만 것이다.

그는 "너의 색시 달아난다" 하는 말을 제일 무서워했다 한다. 한번은 어느 선생이 장난의 말로,

"요즘 같은 따뜻한 봄날엔 옛날부터 색시들이 달아나기를 좋아하는데 어제도 저 아랫말에서 둘이나 달아났다니까 오늘은 이 동리에서 꼭 달아나는 색시가 있을걸……."

했더니 수건이는 점심을 먹다 말고 눈이 휘둥그레졌다 한다. 그리고 그날 오후에는 어서 바삐 하학을 시키고 집으로 갈 양으로 오십 분 만에 치는 종을 이십 분 만에,

The most unsettling thing to tell him was, "Your woman's going to run away from you."

One day a teacher had facetiously told him, "You know, ever since the old days, women have always preferred warm spring days like this for running away from their husbands. I heard a couple of ladies in the village down yonder flew the coop yesterday. I wouldn't be surprised if it happened in our neighborhood today..."

Su-gŏn had stopped in the middle of his lunch and looked up at the teacher wide-eyed in surprise. That afternoon, wanting to go home early, he rang the school bell every twenty minutes instead of the usual fifty minutes. So the story went.

I had practically forgotten about Su-gŏn when one day he paid us a visit.

"Mr. Yi?"

I was delighted to see him.

"Any problems with the delivery of your paper, sir?"

He sounded as if he were now in charge of newspaper delivery.

"No. Why?"

"It always comes right on time?"

삼십 분 만에 함부로 다가서 쳤다는 이야기도 있다.

　하루는 나는 거의 그를 잊어버리고 있을 때,

　"이 선생님 곕쇼?"

하고 수건이가 찾아왔다. 반가웠다.

　"선생님, 요즘 신문이 걸르지 않고 잘 옵쇼?"

하고 그는 배달 감독이나 되어 온 듯이 묻는다.

　"잘 오, 왜 그류?"

한즉 또,

　"늦지도 않굽쇼, 일쯕이 제때마다 꼭꼭 옵쇼?"

한다.

　"당신이 돌 때보다 세 시간은 일쯕이 오고 날마다

꼭꼭 잘 오."

하니 그는 머리를 벅적벅적 긁으면서,

　"하루라도 걸르기만 해라. 신문사에 가서 대뜸 일러바

치지……."

하고 그 빈약한 주먹을 부르댄다.

　"그런뎁쇼, 선생님?"

　"왜 그류?"

"Yes, every day—and three hours earlier than when you delivered it."

Hwang scratched his head sheepishly.

"Well, if it's ever held up, I'll go straight to the office and give them what for," he said, brandishing his puny fist. "You know what, sir?"

"What?"

"The errand boy who came after me at Samsan School—do you think he's stronger than me?"

"Well, I haven't seen him, so I can't say."

He smiled genially.

"I'm going to get that job back, and I got a few angles I'm playing," he said in an earnest tone.

"What angles, if I may ask?"

"It's a snap—I'll go to the school office every day and pester them to take me back. And you know what—the new guy is a lot bigger than me. And he's been grumbling about me. That means we're going to have a showdown. So I'd better see how strong he is."

He chuckled.

"Darn right," I said. "If you challenge him without sizing him up first, you'll catch a beating."

Su-gŏn came a step closer and gave me a confidential smile.

"삼산학교에 말씀예요, 그 제 대신 들어온 급사가 저보다 근력이 세게 생겼습죠?"

"나는 그 사람을 보지 못해서 모르겠소."

하니 그는 은근한 말소리로 히죽거리며,

"제가 거길 또 들어가 볼랴굽쇼, 운동을 합죠."

한다.

"어떻게 운동을 하오?"

"그까짓 거 날마당 사무실로 갑죠. 다시 써달라고 졸라 댑죠. 아, 그랬더니 새 급사란 녀석이 저보다 크기도 무척 큰뎁쇼, 이 녀석이 막 불근댑니다그려. 그래 한번 쌈을 해야 할 턴뎁쇼, 그 녀석이 근력이 얼마나 센지 알아야 뎀벼들 턴뎁쇼…… 허."

"그렇지, 멋모르고 대들었다 매만 맞지."

하니 그는 한 걸음 다가서며 또 은근한 말을 한다.

"그래섭쇼, 엊저녁엔 큰 돌멩이 하나를 굴려다 삼산학교 대문에다 놨습죠. 그리구 오늘 아침에 가보니간 없어졌는뎁쇼. 이 녀석이 나처럼 억지루 굴려다 버렸는지, 뻔쩍 들어다 버렸는지 그만 못 봤거든입쇼, 제―길……."

하고 머리를 긁는다. 그러더니 갑자기 무얼 생각한 듯

"You're right. So, last night I rolled a big rock up to the front gate of the school. This morning it was gone. But since I didn't see him, I can't tell if he rolled it like I did, or if he picked it up easy as can be. Dang!"

He scratched his head again. Then, as if he had suddenly thought of something, he clapped his hands.

"I almost forgot—the real reason I came was to tell you not to get a smallpox vaccination."

"Why shouldn't I?"

"Well, the pox is going around, and everybody's getting vaccinated. But if you're vaccinated against smallpox, you lose your strength," he said, rolling up his sleeve and showing me his vaccination mark. "Look at this. I was vaccinated, and now I'm not as strong as I used to be."

"Who told you all this?"

"I figured it out myself," he said with a grin.

"Yes?" I said, waiting for an explanation.

"Well...Pockmark Yun, who lives down yonder—he's strong as an ox. He was never vaccinated, you know. That new guy at Samsan School—he'll be a pushover if he's been vaccinated."

"I'm very grateful to you for passing on this clever

손뼉을 탁 치더니,

"그런뎁쇼, 제가 온 건입쇼, 댁에선 우두[3]를 넣지 마시라구 왔습죠."

한다.

"우두를 왜 넣지 말란 말이오?"

한즉,

"요즘 마마가 다닌다구 모두 우두들을 넣는뎁쇼, 우두를 넣으면 사람이 근력이 없어지는 법인뎁쇼."

하고 자기 팔을 걷어 올려 우두 자리를 보이면서,

"이걸 봅쇼. 저두 우두를 이렇게 넣었기 때문에 근력이 줄었습죠."

한다.

"우두를 넣으면 근력이 준다고 누가 그립디까?"

물으니 그는 싱글거리며,

"아, 제가 생각해 냈습죠."

한다.

"왜 그렇소?"

하고 캐니,

"뭘…… 저 아래 윤금보라고 있는데 기운이 장산뎁쇼. 아 삼산학교 그 녀석두 우두만 넣었다면 그까짓 것

idea."

He beamed contentedly and scratched his head.

"Are you still waiting for them to take you back at the school?"

"Naw. If I had some money, I wouldn't bother my head about being a worthless errand boy. With some capital I could walk tall and set up a shop in front of the school."

"What would you sell?"

"Well, until summer vacation I'd sell *ch'amoe* melons, and in the fall, roasted chestnuts, Japanese rice cakes, calligraphy paper, drawing paper—you name it. You know, the pupils there think more highly of me than they do the teachers."

That day I gave him three *wŏn* and told him to do as he said—to "walk tall" and set up a melon stand in front of the school. I told him not to worry about repayment if he couldn't turn a profit.

He rushed out the gate, practically dancing in his delight, and was gone. The next day he dropped by while I was out and left three *ch'amoe* melons with my wife, asking her to offer them to me.

But we didn't see hide nor hair of him the whole summer.

I heard later that he had set up his melon stand

무서울 것 없는뎁쇼, 그걸 모르겠거든입쇼……."

한다. 나는,

"그렇게 용한 생각을 하고 일러주러 왔으니 아주 고맙소."

하였다. 그는 좋아서 벙긋거리며 머리를 긁었다.

"그래 삼산학교에 다시 들기만 기다리고 있소?"

물으니 그는,

"돈만 있으면 그까짓 거 누가 고스까이[4] 노릇을 합쇼. 밑천만 있으면 삼산학교 앞에 가서 뻐젓이 장사를 할 턴뎁쇼."

한다.

"무슨 장사?"

"아, 방학 될 때까지 차미 장사도 하굽쇼, 가을부턴 군밤 장사, 왜떡 장사, 습자지, 도화지 장사 막 합죠. 삼산학교 학생들이 저를 어떻게 좋아하겝쇼. 저를 선생들보다 낫게 치는뎁쇼."

한다.

나는 그날 그에게 돈 삼 원을 주었다. 그의 말대로 삼산학교 앞에 가서 뻐젓이 참외 장사라도 해 보라고. 그리고 돈은 남지 못하면 돌려오지 않아도 좋다 하였다.

only to see the monsoon rains set in shortly thereafter. That's when melons lose their taste, and soon his capital was exhausted. But this development paled in comparison with the shocking news that his wife had abandoned him. She and Su-gŏn had gotten along well enough, but she could no longer put up with the ill treatment she suffered at the hands of his sister-in-law. If Su-gŏn had been a normal man, they might have been able to live in a house of their own someday, and she could have waited for that. But the prospect of living out her days under the sister-in-law's thumb had prompted her to leave.

Then one night a few days ago, Su-gŏn visited for the first time in about a month. He was armed with half a dozen bunches of large grapes. I noticed he hadn't bothered to wrap them in paper.

"For you, sir," he said with a broad smile.

Just then somebody came up from behind, grabbed him firmly by the collar, and dragged him off. Su-gŏn's dimwitted face turned pale, and he offered no resistance as he was led away. I guessed immediately that he had stolen the grapes from the vineyard. I followed the two men, stepped in between them as Su-gŏn was being beaten, and offered to

그는 삼 원 돈에 덩실덩실 춤을 추다시피 뛰어나갔다.
그리고 그 이튿날,

　"선생님 잡수시라굽쇼."

하고 나 없는 때 참외 세 개를 갖다 두고 갔다.

　그러고는 온 여름 동안 그는 우리 집에 얼른하지[5] 않
았다.

　들으니 참외 장사를 해보긴 했는데 이내 장마가 들어
밑천만 까먹었고, 또 그까짓 것보다 한 가지 놀라운 소
식은 그의 아내가 달아났단 것이다. 저희끼리 금슬은
괜찮았건만 동서가 못 견디게 굴어 달아난 것이라 한
다. 남편만 남 같으면 따로 살림 나는 날이나 기다리고
살 것이나 평생 동서 밑에 살아야 할 신세를 생각하고
달아난 것이라 한다.

　그런데 요 며칠 전이었다. 밤인데 달포 만에 수건이가
우리 집을 찾아왔다. 웬 포도를 큰 것으로 대여섯 송이
를 종이에 싸지도 않고 맨손에 들고 들어왔다. 그는 벙
긋거리며 첫마디로,

　"선생님 잡수라고 사 왔습죠."

하는 때였다. 웬 사람 하나가 날쌔게 그의 뒤를 따라 들
어오더니 다짜고짜로 수건이의 멱살을 움켜쥐고 끌고

pay for the grapes. In the meantime Su-gŏn man-
aged to slip away.

I took the grapes home, set them on the table,
and stared at them as I nibbled a few. For the longest time I rolled each of them in my mouth, as if
to savor the fruit of Su-gŏn's warm-hearted naive-
te.

Last night I returned late from downtown. I could
see no lights as I passed through Seongbuk-dong;
there was only the luxuriant moonlight brightening
the road.

As I made my way up the hill near the vineyard, I
heard a raspy voice.

"Sa...ke...wa...na...midaka, tamei...ki...ka."[1]

A man was coming down the hill. The way he
swung his arms as he walked made the wide road
seem narrow. I looked closer; it appeared to be
Su-gŏn. Knowing he would be embarrassed if I
called out to him and he saw it was me, I quickly
hid myself in the shade of a tree at the side of the
road.

He stared up at the moon, not looking at the
road, and kept repeating the same words from the

나갔다. 수건이는 그 우둔한 얼굴이 새하얗게 질리며 꼼짝 못 하고 끌려 나갔다.

나는 수건이가 포도원에서 포도를 훔쳐온 것을 직각하였다. 쫓아 나가 매를 말리고 포돗값을 물어주었다. 포돗값을 물어주고 보니 수건이는 어느 틈에 사라지고 보이지 않았다.

나는 그 다섯 송이의 포도를 탁자 위에 얹어놓고 오래 바라보며 아껴 먹었다. 그의 은근한 순정의 열매를 먹듯 한 알을 가지고도 오래 입 안에 굴려보며 먹었다.

어제다. 문안에 들어갔다 늦어서 나오는데 불빛 없는 성북동 길 위에는 밝은 달빛이 깁[6]을 깐 듯하였다.

그런데 포도원께를 올라오노라니까 누가 맑지도 못한 목청으로,

"사…… 께…… 와 나…… 미다까 다메이……
끼…… 까……."[7]

를 부르며 큰길이 좁다는 듯이 휘적거리며 내려왔다. 보니까 수건이 같았다. 나는,

"수건인가?"

song. Perhaps that first line was the only line he knew. And he was puffing away on a cigarette—something I'd never seen him do before.

To Su-gŏn too, a moonlit night called forth all sorts of sentiments.

1) "Teardrops and sighs"; from a Japanese song popular in Korea at the time.

* From *A Ready-Made Life,* ed. and trans. Kim Chong-un and Bruce Fulton (Honolulu: University of Hawai'i Press, 1998), 46-54. Translation copyright © 1998 by Kim Chong-un and Bruce Fulton. Used by permission from University of Hawai'i Press. All Rights Reserved. Not for reproduction.

Translated by Kim Chong-un and Bruce Fulton

하고 아는 체하려다 그가 나를 보면 무안해할 일이 있는 것을 생각하고 획 길 아래로 내려서 나무 그늘에 몸을 감추었다.

그는 길은 보지도 않고 달만 쳐다보며, 노래는 그 이상은 외우지도 못하는 듯 첫 줄 한 줄만 되풀이하면서 전에는 본 적이 없었는데 담배를 다 퍽퍽 빨면서 지나갔다.

달밤은 그에게도 유감한 듯하였다.

1) 핫삐. 등에 상호를 박은 겉옷을 뜻하는 일본어. 핫피.
2) 반편. 지능이 보통 사람보다 모자라는 사람을 낮잡아 이르는 말. 반편이.
3) 우두. 천연두를 예방하기 위하여 소에서 뽑은 면역 물질.
4) 고스까이. '급사', '심부름꾼'을 뜻하는 일본말.
5) 얼른하다. 얼씬하다.
6) 깁. 명주실로 바탕을 조금 거칠게 짠 비단.
7) 술은 눈물인가 한숨인가.

  * 작가 고유의 문체나 당시 쓰이던 용어를 그대로 살려 원문에
    최대한 가깝게 표기하고자 하였다. 단, 현재 쓰이지 않는 말이
    나 띄어쓰기는 현행 맞춤법에 맞게 표기하였다.

《중앙(中央)》, 1933

해설

Afterword

동정과 연민의 시선

강진호 (문학평론가)

소설은 허구의 창조이다. 허구의 창조이되, 인물을 통해서 구체적인 성격을 창조하는 것을 중요한 목표로 삼는다. 현대소설을 쓰는 작가가 최고의 목표로 삼는 것은 '참다우면서도 온당한 인물의 창조'일 것이다. 이태준은 누구보다도 그런 명제에 충실했던 작가였다. '오몽녀' '기생 산월이' '손거부' '영월영감' '색시' 등과 같이 작중인물이 작품의 제목이 될 정도로 인물을 소설의 핵심요소로 중시했던 것이다. 이태준은 간결하고 정확한 문장을 바탕으로 특유의 감성적 분위기를 만들어 인물의 성격을 창조해 냈다. 그는 형용사 하나하나의 정확성을 따졌고 한번 완성한 문장도 몇 번이나 고치는 결벽증에

A Sympathetic and Compassionate Gaze

Kang Jin-ho (literary critic)

Fiction is a creation of the imagination. Its crucial objective is to create specific personalities through the formation of characters. The most important objective of modern fiction writers is probably the creation of a true and reasonable character. Yi T'ae-jun was devoted to and a master of that goal. He placed a great emphasis on characters as the main elements of fiction—the titles of his works are the names of their main characters—"Omongnyŏ," "*Ki-saeng* Sanwŏl," "Son Kŏbu (Millionaire Son)," "Yŏngwol Yŏnggam (Old Man from Yŏngwol)," and "Saeksi (New Bride)."

Using accurate and concise sentences, Yi created

가까운 문장 의식을 갖고 있었다. 그렇게 다듬어진 문장으로 인물의 성격을 포착해 낸 관계로 작품은 마치 영화를 보는 듯한 실감을 제공한다.

「달밤」은 이태준의 그러한 특성을 전형적으로 보여주는 작품이다. 소설은 크게 두 부분으로 구성되어 있다. 하나는 성북동으로 이사 온 뒤 우연히 알게 된 황수건의 내력이고, 다른 하나는 장사에 실패하고 또 아내마저 달아난 뒤 실의에 빠진 황수건에 대한 나(화자)의 동정과 연민의 태도이다. 먼저, 주인공 황수건은 화자가 이사 온 곳이 시골임을 실감나게 해준 인물로, 쨍구 머리에다가 손과 팔목이 작고 가느다란 우둔하고 모자라기까지 한 '못난이'로 그려진다. 그런 특성으로 인해 그는 삼산학교 급사로 있다가 쫓겨났고 지금은 신문사 보조 배달부로 일하지만 그마저도 위태로운 처지에 놓인다. 이 '반편이' 인물에 대해 화자는 시종일관 애정과 관심을 보여서 관조하고 응시하는 태도를 유지한다. 그러다가 새 배달부가 채용되면서 황수건은 보조배달부에서 떨려나고 한동안 나타나지 않는 상황이 되자, 화자는 '섭섭'뿐 아니라 '마음이 아프기'까지 하다. 이런 순박한 인물마저 용납하지 못하는 세상의 야박함에 대한 원

personalities by establishing unique emotional moods. He was compulsive about his sentences, to the point that he calculated the accuracy of every adjective, and repeatedly revised his work. Because he captured the personalities of characters in such carefully crafted sentences, his works comes alive, like movies.

The story "An Idiot's Delight" is emblematic of Yi T'ae-jun's writing. This short fiction consists of two main parts: the first is Hwang Su-gŏn's story, which the narrator finds out by chance after moving to Seongbuk-dong. The second is the narrator's sympathetic and compassionate attitude toward Hwang, who is living in despair after his wife has left him. First, the protagonist Hwang Su-gŏn fills the narrator with the feeling that he is truly in rustic surroundings. Hwang is portrayed as an obtuse and slow-witted "simpleton" with a large bulging head and small hands and wrists. Because of his condition, he was laid off from Sansam Primary School, where he worked as an errand boy, and is delivering newspapers not as a regular carrier but as a helper. However, even that job is on the line. Throughout the story, the narrator maintains a consistently contemplative and observing attitude, showing his

47

망을 표현하는 것이다.

　후반부는 이 황수건을 거의 잊고 있던 화자 앞에 황수건이 다시 나타나면서 시작된다. 화자는 황수건을 반기면서 실없는 이야기를 주고받다가 황수건이 삼산학교 앞에서 장사를 하고 싶다는 말을 듣고는 돈을 주어 장사를 해보라고 한다. 화자는 이제 단순한 이야기의 서술자가 아니라 스스로 작품에 등장하는 인물이다. 지켜보기만 하던 화자가 인물의 삶에 개입해서 동정과 연민의 태도를 행동으로 표현한 것이다. 황수건은 그 돈으로 참외장사를 하지만 바로 망하고 게다가 아내까지 달아나는 상황에 처한다. 동서와 사이가 좋지 않았고 평생 그 동서 밑에서 살 것을 생각하고는 달아났다는 것. 그러던 어느 날 황수건은 화자의 고마움에 감사를 표시하듯이 포도송이 대여섯을 갖다 주는데, 알고 보니 그것은 포도원에서 훔친 것이었다. 주인에게 포도 값을 물어준 뒤 화자는 '은근한 순정의 열매'를 먹듯이 포도송이를 음미한다. 얼마 후 화자는 달밤에 황수건이 '술은 눈물인가, 한숨인가~'라는 노래를 부르며 담배를 퍽퍽 빨고 지나가는 모습을 목격한다.

　이런 내용을 통해서 작가는 한 사람의 개성적인 인물

care and interest in this "half-wit." When a new paperboy takes over the delivery and Hwang Su-gŏn
stops coming to the narrator's house, the narrator
feels "heartache" and expresses his resentment at
the world's heartless treatment of this simple man.

The second part of the story begins with Hwang
Su-gŏn's surprise visit to the narrator, who had almost forgotten about him. The narrator welcomes
Hwang and while making idle conversation, Hwang
mentions that he wants to set up shop in front of
Samsan Primary School. The narrator gives him
some money and tells him to start his business. At
this point, the narrator enters the story as an active
character, no longer simply a narrator. He turns into
a character who intervenes in the life of another
character and physically expresses his sympathetic
and compassionate attitude toward him. With the
money the narrator has given him, Hwang begins to
sell melons. Soon, though, he goes out of business
and even his wife leaves him, because she can't
abide the prospect of living out her days under her
sister-in-law's rule. Then, one day, Hwang brings
home half a dozen bunches of grapes, which turn
out to have been stolen from a vineyard. After he
pays for the grapes, the narrator rolls them in his

을 창조해 내고, 동시에 현실에 대한 비판적 인식을 드러내었다. 황수건은 현실과의 관계가 조화롭지 못한 인물이다. 그는 현실의 거대한 힘에 밀려서 세상의 뒷전으로 내몰린 무기력한 인물이다. 태고적 사람과도 같이 순진한 황수건은 그런 모습으로 인해 주변 사람들로부터 무시를 당하는데, 이는 순박한 어린이들을 가르치며 살겠다는 소박한 꿈마저 좌절되고 마는 「실낙원 이야기」의 K 교사처럼, 추구하는 삶의 가치가 현실과의 거리가 먼 까닭이다. 이러한 인물들을 통해 상허는 그들의 소박한 꿈마저 용납하지 못하는 현실에 실망하고 때로는 분노를 표현한다. 그렇지만 이태준은 그런 사실을 결코 직설적 화법으로 드러내지 않는다. 그는 문학은 언어 예술이라는 자각에 투철했고, 그래서 그런 의도를 감각적 분위기와 소설적 형상을 통해서 제시한다. 희미하게 달이 비추는 밤, '술은 눈물인가, 한숨인가~'라는 유행가를 부르면서 담배를 '퍽퍽' 빨고 비틀거리는 황수건의 모습, 이태준 소설이 갖는 중요한 매력의 하나는 이렇듯 정교한 묘사를 통해서 독특한 분위기와 풍경을 창출한 데 있다. 이재선이나 정한숙이 상허를 두고 "단편소설의 완성자" "단편소설의 기법을 완벽하게 체득한

mouth to "savor the fruit of Hwang's warm-hearted naiveté." A few nights later, the narrator sees Hwang walking by, puffing on a cigarette and contentedly singing "Teardrops and Sighs."

Through his storytelling, the author creates an individual with a unique personality. At the same time, he reveals his critical view of the reality. Hwang Su-gŏn is a person who does not fit in. He is a torpid individual who has been pushed to the back by the immense power of social reality. His naiveté, like that of people throughout the ages, prompts others to spurn him. The reason is that the value of the life he pursues is far from reality (similar to the teacher K in "Story of Paradise Lost"). Through these characters, Yi expresses his disappointment and sometimes anger at the reality that cannot allow such people to realize their simple dreams. However, he doesn't do so in direct speech. He had a clear understanding of literature as the art of language, and therefore expressed his motives and intentions through a melancholy mood and format, as in the image of Hwang Su-gŏn singing while puffing on a cigarette and swaggering under the luxuriant moonlight. One of the startling charms that Yi T'ae-jun's works display is creating a unique

작가"라고 평했던 것은 인물의 성격이나 분위기를 창출해 내는 이런 특성을 두고 한 말이었다. 그리고 바로 이런 점이 문학적 자율성에 대한 상허의 믿음과 의지를 보여주는 대목이다. 문학을 사회운동의 수단이나 계몽의 도구로 보지 않고 오직 언어의 아름다움과 개성적 묘사에서 찾는 그의 태도는 이광수나 프로작가들과는 다른 근대적 예술인의 모습을 보여주는 것이었다.

mood and scenery, as well as personalities, through such detailed descriptions. This is why Lee Chae-sŏn and Chŏng Han-suk described Yi T'ae-jun as the "perfector of short stories" and a writer "who perfectly mastered the technique of short-story writing." This characteristic also reflects Yi's trust and confidence in literary autonomy. He didn't view literature as a means of achieving a social movement or as a tool of enlightenment. Instead, Yi T'ae-jun, who found linguistic and descriptive beauty in literature, was a modern artist, and as such different from Yi Kwang-su and Proletariat literature camp writers.

비평의 목소리

Critical Acclaim

이태준 씨의 「달밤」은 나를 앙분(昻奮)시키고 고통과 애감(哀感)을 채워 주었다. 그리하여 끝내는 나를 울리고야 말았다. 나의 눈물을 센티멘털하고 값싼 눈물이라고 조소할 사람이 있을는지도 모르겠으나 나는 조금도 나의 흘린 눈물이 부끄럽지 않다. 나는 이 「달밤」 속에서 애달프고 괴롭고 추악한 인생을 보았다. 어찌 내가 흘린 눈물이 부끄러울 것이냐? 눈물은 결코 '창조의 부정'은 아니다. 괴롭고 안타깝고 괴로울 때 흘린 눈물이 얼마나 우리의 영(靈)을 정화하여 주며 정신을 고양시켜 주느냐? 얼마나 험하고 괴로움 많은 인생에 돌아갈 새로운 용기를 부어주느냐? 그렇다. 진정한 예술은 언

Yi T'ae-jun's "An Idiot's Delight" disturbed me and filled me with a sense of suffering and sorrow. And, in the end, it made me cry. Some people might mock me, saying that my tears are sentimental and cheap, but I am not ashamed of them. In this story, I witnessed a heartrending, distressed, and hideous life. So why should I be ashamed of my tears? Tears do not symbolize a *denial of creation*. Don't the tears we shed in pain and sorrow cleanse our souls and lift up our spirits? Don't they encourage us anew to return to our lives, which are so full of rough days and sufferings? They do. True art has always brought tears to our eyes. Yet, instead of

제나 우리를 울렸다. 그러면서도 우리를 눈물에 침닉(沈溺)하여 실망 낙첨(落膽)하고 자포자기하게 하지 않고 새로운 희망과 용기를 가지고 인생에 돌아가게 하였다.

김환태, 「상허의 작품과 그 예술관」, 《개벽》, 1934.12

인간상을 묘출하는 데 이태준만큼 명확한 수완을 가진 작가도 드물께다. 그는 인물을 그리되 수다스럽지 않고 또 구태여 그 인물의 내면생활로 들어가 무슨 비밀을 끌어내려고도 하지 않는다. 스켓취적 필치로 그 인물의 말이나 행동을 점점이 탓치하여 가는 동안에 어언간 선명한 인간상이 나타난다. 만일 이씨의 인물 묘사의 비밀이 있다면 그것은 그들에 대한 부절한 흥미와 동정 그것뿐일 것이다. 이씨의 작품 인물은 다만 선명할 뿐만은 아니다. 보드랍고 따뜻한 것이 또 그 매력의 일면이다. 그것은 그들에 유-모아와 페이소스가 있기 때문이다. 하잘것없는 인물들의 평평범범(平平凡凡)한 생활 가운데 흐르고 있는 유-모아와 페이소스, 그것을 포착하여 놓는 작자의 명확한 수법—이것이 이태준 단편의 매력이었다.

최재서, 「최근 문단의 동향」, 《조광》, 1937.11

making us fall into despair, disappointed and drowning in tears, it helps us to return to our lives with renewed hope and courage.

Kim Hwan-t'ae, "Yi T'ae-jun's Works and His View of Art," *K'aebyŏk* [Enlightenment], Dec. 1934

Not many writers can match Yi T'ae-jun in his ability to depict human characters. He creates personalities without being wordy, and he doesn't attempt to draw some secret out of them by delving into their psyches. Instead, he sketches them through their own words and actions—and clear-cut characters appear. If there is a secret to how Yi depicts his characters, it is probably his incessant interest and sympathy toward them. They are not just vivid, but also soft and warm, which comes from their sense of humor and pathos—the humor and pathos that wind through the lives of common people. The precise way in which he captures them is the charm of Yi T'ae-jun's short stories.

Choi Chae-sŏ, "The Trend of Contemporary Literary World," *Chogwang*, Nov. 1937

From "Omongnyŏ" to the "Story of a Rabbit," one element runs through Yi's stories: his obsession

「오몽녀」에서 「토끼 이야기」에 이르기까지의 그의 작품을 일관하는 것은 소설에서의 언어, 혹은 그것들의 집적물인 언어의 형식미에 대한 집착이라 할 수 있다. 그는 이야기하려는 것보다 이야기하는 방법에 대하여 보다 더 많은 예술적 성취도를 두고 있는 듯하다. 그의 소설이 우리에게 제시하고 있는 아름다움이란 그 이야기 자체의 짜임새에 있는 것이었지 그러한 이야기를 가능케 했던 현실 세계와의 조응을 통한 아름다움이 아니라는 점은 중요하다. 그의 소설에서의 현실 세계란 인물의 근거를 마련해 주기 위한 원경(遠景)으로서의 그것으로 의미 기능을 상실한 부차적인 것으로 밀려나 있다. 따라서 그의 소설이 환기시켜 주는 아름다움이란 구체적이고 일상적인 삶의 올과 결에 맞닿아 있지 않는, 막연한 애수나 정조 또는 분위기로서의 그것이라는 데 한계가 있다.

서종택, 「이태준의 단편소설」, 「한국현대소설연구」

새문사, 1990.5

with the language of fiction, or the formal beauty of language. Artistically, he seems to lay more emphasis on delivering his stories than on their contents. It is important to understand that the beauty in his works lies in the weave of the story and not in the consonance of the story and the reality that made it possible. In Yi's fiction, reality has lost its function as providing the basis for the characters—reality has become a minor element. As a result, the beauty that his fiction arouses is limited, as it is not embedded in the detailed fabric of everyday lives, but rather remains as an indefinable grief, sentiment, or mood.

Sŏ Chong-t'aek, "Yi T'ae-jun's Short Stories,"

Studies on Modern Korean Novels, (Seoul: Saemunsa, 1990)

이태준

이태준은 1904년 11월 4일 강원도 철원군 묘장면 산명리에서 태어났다. 호는 상허(尙虛). 6살 때까지 고향에서 성장한 이태준은 아버지를 따라 블라디보스토크로 이주하였으나 아버지의 사망으로 귀국하고 얼마 후 어머니마저 잃는 비운을 겪는다. 이후 이태준은 친척집을 전전하며 불우한 어린 시절을 보내지만 남다른 강인함과 성취욕으로 봉명학교를 졸업하면서는 전교생을 대표해서 상을 받기도 하였다. 1921년 휘문고보에 입학하였으나 동맹휴교 사건에 연루되어 퇴학을 당했고, 이후 친구 김연만의 도움으로 도일(渡日)하여 상지대(上智大) 예과에 입학한다. 그렇지만 생활고에 시달리다가 1927년 11월 중도 퇴학한 후 귀국했다. 1929년에 '개벽사'에 입사한 뒤《학생》《신생》《어린이》등의 잡지에 관여하면서 많은 양의 수필과 동화를 발표하였다. 1925년《조선문단》에 「오몽녀」가 입선되어 작품 활동을 시작했지만, 일본 유학으로 잠시 주춤하다가 다시 활동을 시작한 것이다. 1933년에는 '구인회(九人會)' 결성을 주도하

Yi T'ae-jun

Yi T'ae-jun was born on November 4, 1904 at Sanmyŏng-*ri* Village in Cheorwon-*gun* District, Gangwon-*do* Province. His penname was Sanghŏ. He grew up in the same village until he was six years old, when he followed his father and moved to Vladivostok. He returned to Korea after his father's death, and lost his mother soon afterwards as well. As a result, Yi T'ae-jun spent his childhood moving from one relative's house to another. However, with remarkable willpower and a desire for accomplishment, Yi received an award on behalf of his classmates at his graduation from Bongmyŏng School. In 1921, he enrolled in Huimun High School, but was expelled later due to his involvement in student strikes. With the help of his friend Kim Yŏn-man, Yi fled to Japan and enrolled in the Arts Program at Sophia University. Unfortunately, he dropped out in November 1927 due to destitution and returned to Korea. In 1929, he started working at Kaebyŏksa and was involved in the production of various periodicals, such as *Student, New Birth,* and

면서 이상, 박태원 등과 함께 프로문학과 구별되는 이른바 순수문학을 주창하였다. 당시 이태준은 《조선중앙일보》의 기자로 있으면서 구인회 작가들을 적극 후원했고, 자신도 활발하게 작품을 발표해서 「꽃나무는 심어놓고」 「달밤」 「색시」 「손거부」 「가마귀」 등 그의 대표작으로 평가되는 일련의 작품들을 발표하였다. 이후 이태준은 예술성이 뛰어난 순수문학 작가이자 단편소설의 완성자라는 평가를 듣는다. 1939년에는 종합 문예지 《문장》을 주재하면서 전통에 깊은 관심을 보였고, 신인 발굴에도 앞장서서 임옥인, 곽하신, 최태응 등을 배출하였다. 하지만 1940년대를 넘기면서 일제의 침략전쟁이 본격화되자 이태준은 1943년 6월 『왕자호동』을 마지막으로 절필한 뒤 철원으로 낙향하였다.

철원에서 해방 소식을 접한 이태준은 "코허리가 찌르르"한 감격을 느끼고 바로 상경하여 임화, 김남천 등과 함께 '조선문학건설본부'를 주도하면서 이전과는 확연히 다른 행보를 보여주었다. 「해방전후」에서 언급되듯이, 이전의 '소극적인 처세'에서 벗어나 '의연히 일해야 할 공간'으로 해방기를 받아들이고, '민주주의 민족전선'의 문화부장, 《현대일보》의 주간 등을 역임하면서 정치

Children. During that time, he published many essays and children's stories. He began to write his maturer works after his debut in 1925 with "Omongnyŏ," which won the *Chosŏn Mundan* competition. After a short break due to studies in Japan, Yi resumed his writing career. In 1933, he formed Kuinhoe [Circle of Nine] and advocated the so-called "pure litera-ture" along with Yi Sang and Pak Taewon, as op-posed to proletariat literature. As a reporter at *Chosŏn Chungang Ilbo,* he vigorously supported writers in Kuinhoe and also published a series of his own works, including "Kkotnamunŭn simŏnoko [After Planting Flower Trees]," "Saeksi [New Bride]," "Son Kŏbu [Millionaire Son]," and "Kkamagui [Crows]," which are considered to be some of his best. From then, Yi T'ae-jun was acclaimed as an outstanding pure literature writer and a "perfector of short stories." In 1939, he showed a great deal of interest in tradition, as the founder of *Munjang* [Sentence], a comprehensive literary magazine, and made efforts to discover talented new writers, such as Im Ok-in, Kwak Ha-sin, and Choi T'ae-ŭng. Yet in the 1940s, as it became clear that Japan was car-rying out a war of aggression, Yi finished writing *Wangja Hodong (Prince Hodong),* in June 1943 and

활동에 적극 가담하였다. 월북 후 이태준은 소련파의
후원을 받으면서 소련을 다녀오고(그 체험담을 기록한 책
이 『소련기행』이다), 전쟁 기간 중에는 종군작가로 참전하
여 인민군 전사들을 격려하는 등 북한의 선전 일꾼으로
적극 활동하였다. 그렇지만 김일성의 체제 정비과정에
서 1955년 소련파와 함께 숙청되는 비극을 맞는다. 1955
년 조선문학예술총동맹 위원장 한설야 등으로부터 공
개적인 비판을 당한 뒤 《함남일보》교정원으로 추방되
었다가 1957년에는 함흥 콘크리트 블록 공장의 노동자
로 강제 배치되었고, 1964년 한때 중앙당 문화부 대남
심리전 참모부 창작실 전속작가로 평양으로 소환되었
다고 한다. 불행하게도 아직껏 그의 사망 연대는 확인
되지 않고 있다.

moved to Cheowon.

Yi received the news of the liberation of Korea from Japanese rule in Cheorwon, which made his "nose and waist twinge" with emotion. Immediately, he moved back to Seoul and led the Chosŏn Literature Building Headquarters, starting a completely different path of life. As mentioned in "Haebang chŏnhu [Before and After Liberation]," he broke away from "passive conduct" and accepted the Liberation as a "space where he must work with fortitude." As the Cultural Director of Democratic People's Front and chief editor of *Hyŏndae Ilbo*, he participated in political activities. After he defected to North Korea, Yi visited the Soviet Union, sponsored by the Soviet Union Group within North Korea. He recorded his experience in his book *A Trip to the Soviet Union*. During the Korean War, he participated in the war as a writer to encourage the soldiers of the Korean People's Army and actively engaged in North Korea's propaganda activities. However, in the process of working in the Kim Il-sung administration, Yi was banished along with the Soviet Union Group in 1955. After he was publicly criticized by Han Seol-ya, the head of the General Federation of Korean Literature and Arts Unions in

1955, he was made to work as a proof-reader at *Hamnam Ilbo*. In 1957, he was forced into labor at a concrete block factory in Hamhŭng. Then some time in 1964, he was called back to Pyongyang as a staff writer of the general staff of Psychological Warfare Against South Korea in the Culture Department of the Central Party. His date of death has not been confirmed yet.

번역 **김종운, 브루스 풀턴**

Translated by Kim Chong-un and Bruce Fulton

故 김종운은 서울대학교, 보든칼리지, 뉴욕대학교에서 수학했으며, 1962년부터 1991년까지 서울대학교에서 영어영문학과에서 학생들을 가르쳤다. 모던 미국문학의 전문가인 그는 솔 벨로와 버나드 맬러머드와 같은 유대 미국인에 대한 폭넓은 글을 썼다. 서울대학교와 한국학술진흥재단에 학장으로 재직한 바 있다. 『전후 한국 단편소설』(개정판, 1983)을 번역하였으며, 『정숙한 여인들: 고전 한국 소설 3』(리차드 러트 공역, 1974), 『레디메이드 인생: 모던 한국 소설의 초기 대가』, (브루스 풀턴 공역, 1998)

The late Kim Chong-un was educated at Seoul National University, Bowdoin College, and New York University. He taught from 1962 to 1991 in the Department of English Language and Literature at Seoul National University. A specialist in modern American literature, he wrote extensively on Jewish American authors such as Saul Bellow and Bernard Malamud. He served as President of Seoul National University and the Korea Research Foundation. He was the translator of *Postwar Korean Short Stories* (revised edition,1983), the co-translator, with Richard Rutt, of *Virtuous Women: Three Classic Korean Novels* (1974), and the co-translator, with Bruce Fulton, of *A Ready-Made Life: Early Masters of Modern Korean Fiction* (1998).

브루스 풀턴은 한국문학 작품을 다수 영역해서 영미권에 소개하고 있다. 『별사-한국 여성 소설가 단편집』 『순례자의 노래-한국 여성의 새로운 글쓰기』 『유형의 땅』 (공역, Marshall R. Pihl)을 번역하였다. 가장 최근 번역한 작품으로는 오정희의 소설집 『불의 강 외 단편소설 선집』, 조정래의 장편소설 『오 하느님』이 있다. 브루스 풀턴은 『레디메이드 인생』(공역, 김종운), 『현대 한국 소설 선집』(공편, 권영민), 『촛농 날개-악타 코리아나 한국 단편 선집』 외 다수의 작품의 번역과 편집을 담당했다. 브루스 풀턴은 서울대학교 국어국문학과에서 박사 학위를 받고 캐나다의 브리티시컬럼비아 대학 민영빈 한국문학 기금 교수로 재직하고 있다. 다수의 번역문학기금과 번역문학상 등을 수상한 바 있다.

Bruce Fulton is the translator of numerous volumes of modern Korean fiction, including the award-winning women's anthologies *Words of Farewell: Stories by Korean Women Writers* (Seal Press, 1989) and *Wayfarer: New Writing by Korean Women* (Women in Translation, 1997), and, with Marshall R. Pihl, *Land of Exile: Contemporary Korean Fiction*, rev. and exp. ed. (M.E. Sharpe, 2007). Their most recent translations are *River of Fire and Other Stories* by O Chŏng-hŭi (Columbia University Press, 2012), and *How in Heaven's Name: A Novel of World War II* by Cho Chŏngnae (MerwinAsia, 2012). Bruce Fulton is co-translator (with Kim Chong-un) of *A Ready-Made Life: Early Masters of Modern Korean Fiction* (University of Hawai'i Press, 1998), co-editor (with Kwon Young-min) of *Modern Korean Fiction: An Anthology* (Columbia University Press, 2005), and editor of *Waxen Wings: The* Acta Koreana *Anthology of Short Fiction From Korea* (Koryo Press, 2011). The Fultons have received several awards and fellowships for their translations, including a National Endowment for the Arts Translation Fellowship, the first ever given for a translation from the Korean, and a residency at the Banff International Literary Translation Centre, the first ever awarded for translators from any Asian language. Bruce Fulton is the inaugural holder of the Young-Bin Min Chair in Korean Literature and Literary Translation, Department of Asian Studies, University of British Columbia.

바이링궐 에디션 한국 대표 소설 098
달밤

2015년 1월 9일 초판 1쇄 발행

지은이 이태준 | 옮긴이 김종운, 브루스 풀턴 | 펴낸이 김재범
기획위원 정은경, 전성태, 이경재 | 편집 정수인, 이은혜, 김형욱, 윤단비 | 관리 박신영
펴낸곳 (주)아시아 | 출판등록 2006년 1월 27일 제406-2006-000004호
주소 서울특별시 동작구 서달로 161-1(흑석동 100-16)
전화 02.821.5055 | 팩스 02.821.5057 | 홈페이지 www.bookasia.org
ISBN 979-11-5662-067-9 (set) | 979-11-5662-075-4 (04810)
값은 뒤표지에 있습니다.

Bi-lingual Edition Modern Korean Literature 098
An Idiot's Delight

Written by Yi T'ae-jun I **Translated by** Kim Chong-un and Bruce Fulton
Published by Asia Publishers I 161-1, Seodal-ro, Dongjak-gu, Seoul, Korea
Homepage Address www.bookasia.org I **Tel**. (822).821.5055 I **Fax**. (822).821.5057
First published in Korea by Asia Publishers 2015
ISBN 979-11-5662-067-9 (set) | 979-11-5662-075-4 (04810)

바이링궐 에디션 한국 대표 소설

한국문학의 가장 중요하고 첨예한 문제의식을 가진 작가들의 대표작을 주제별로 선정!
하버드 한국학 연구원 및 세계 각국의 한국문학 전문 번역진이 참여한 번역 시리즈!
미국 하버드대학교와 컬럼비아대학교 동아시아학과, 캐나다 브리티시컬럼비아대학교 아시아
학과 등 해외 대학에서 교재로 채택!

바이링궐 에디션 한국 대표 소설 set 1

바이링궐 에디션 한국 대표 소설 set 2